THE JOY MARKET

CHILDREN'S PUBLISHING

The Joy Market's books bring joy to the children who read them and to children around the world. All of the money earned from our books goes to causes that directly impact the lives of children.

Join our community that cultivates compassion, creativity & a crazy love for books at

www.thejoymarket.com

Check out a few of our other books

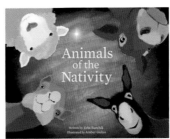

This book was written to honor the children of Syria

You're not a *them*, you're an *us*
And especially to Aylan
Who gave you a face and a name

All the money made from this book will go to relief efforts to serve Syrian children and families who have left their homes in search of safety.

Author: Erin Burchik

Illustrator: Aimee Strickland

Creative Director: Amber Guinn

Copy Editor: Barbara L. Townsend

Special thanks to Brian Burchik for hours of editing and to Matt and Jodi Turner for your support in this project.

First printing, 2015

Printed in the United States of America

THE BEAR HUG

a journey from *them* to *us*

Written by Erin Burchik

Illustrated by Aimee Strickland

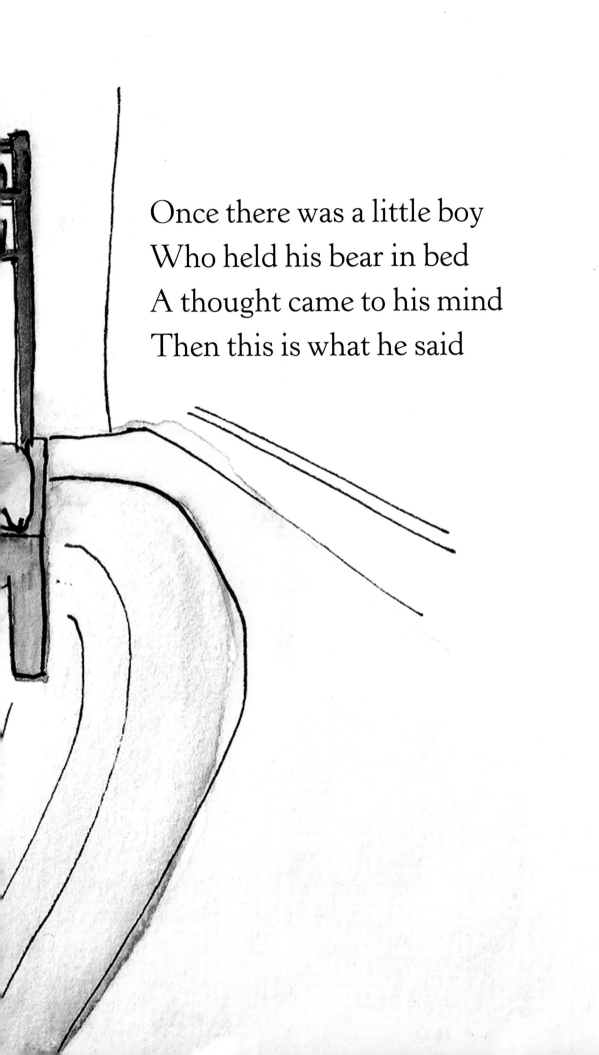

Once there was a little boy
Who held his bear in bed
A thought came to his mind
Then this is what he said

"Mom, I've just been thinking
Of all the kids I know
My friends at school and neighbors
Kids are everywhere I go

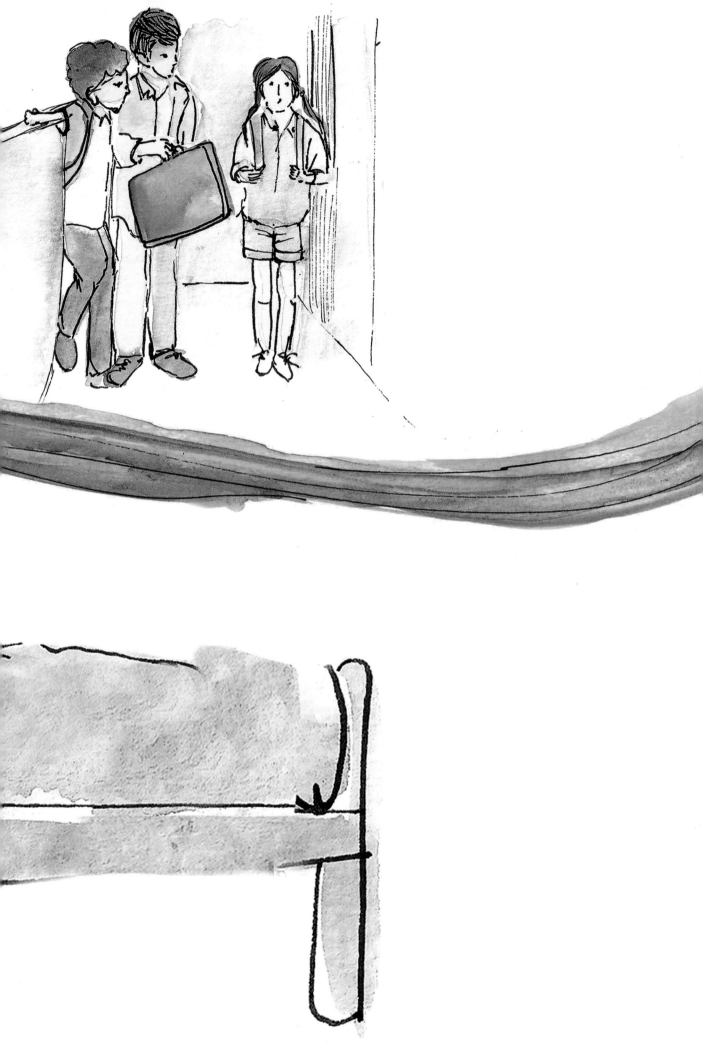

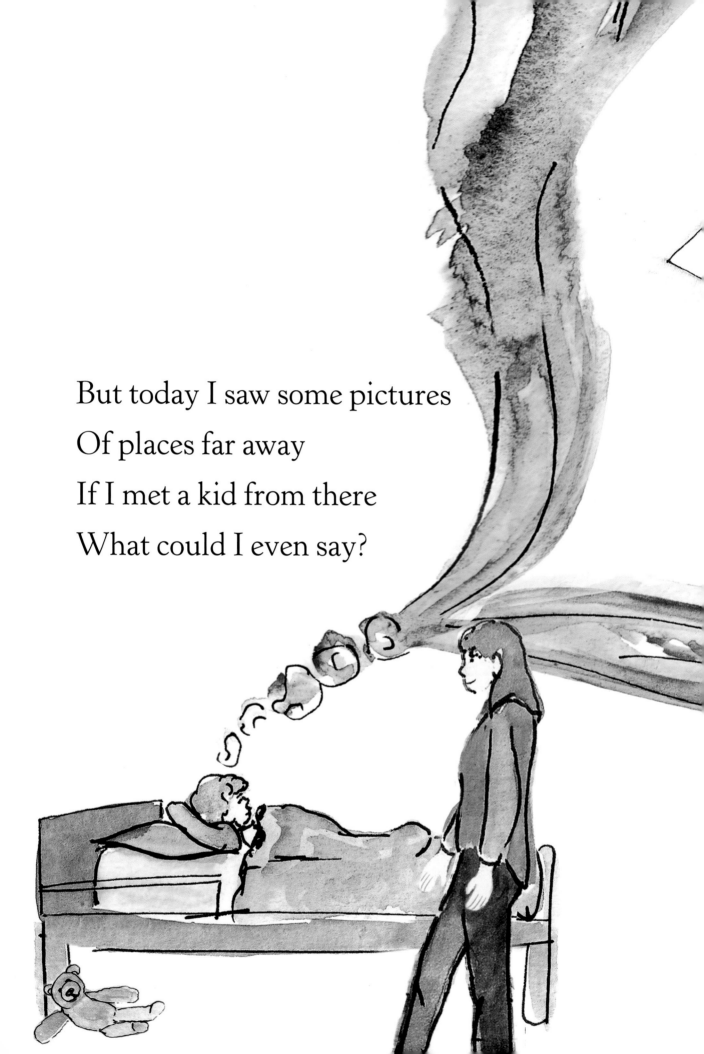

But today I saw some pictures

Of places far away

If I met a kid from there

What could I even say?

We are just too different
There is no way we're the same."
His mom said, "They're each special
And each one has a name

Let's look at this together,"
Then she stood up to walk
She brought a globe to his bed,
Spun it and began to talk

"Son, you would have so much fun
With any kid you met
You speak a common language
That you will never forget

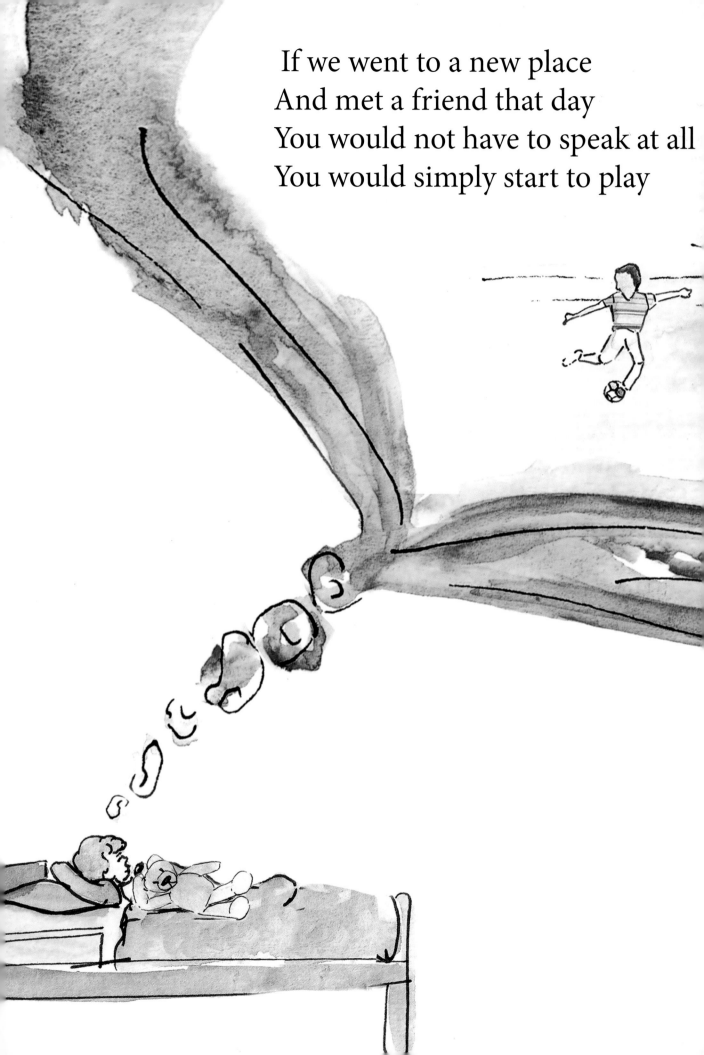

If we went to a new place
And met a friend that day
You would not have to speak at all
You would simply start to play

You might find something round
Like this globe in my hand
And where you stood would be your field
Whether on grass or desert sand

If we went to Mexico
You might kick the ball with José
And after you made a good shot
He could teach you to chant 'Olé!'

But if we went to Kenya
Zuri might ask you to play
She'd show you open spaces
Where you could run all day

If we played ball in India
Your friend Raj might not kick it
But he would be so excited
To teach you to play cricket

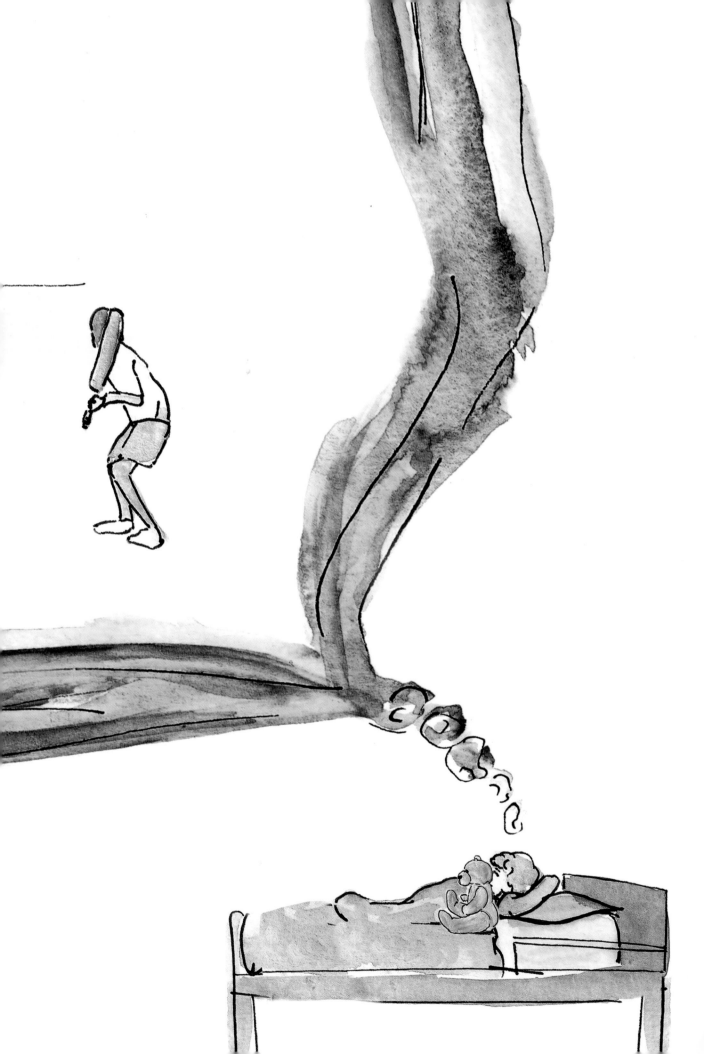

If we traveled to Iraq
Noor would hold a string tight
And she'd let you have a turn
While teaching you to fly a kite

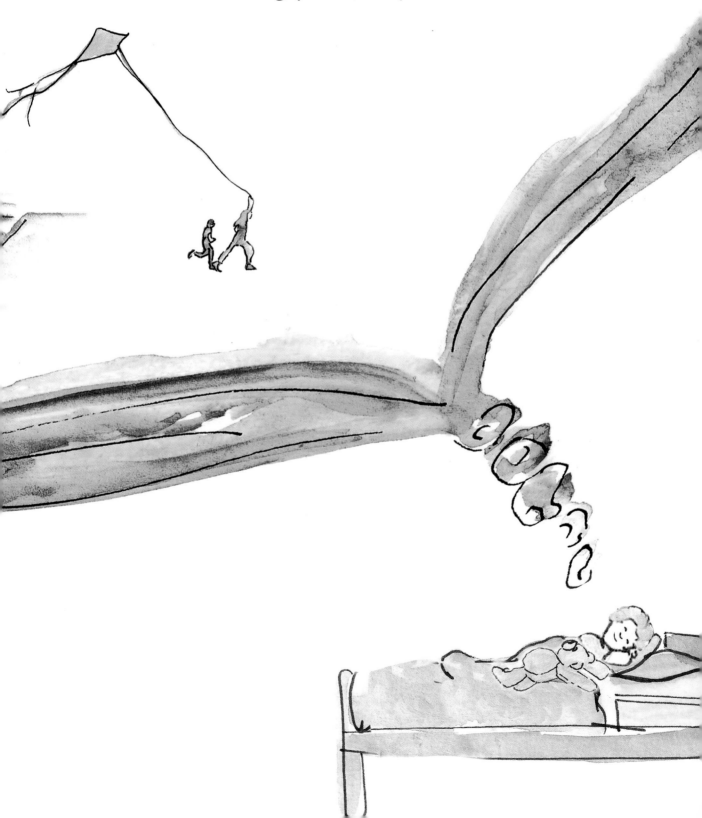

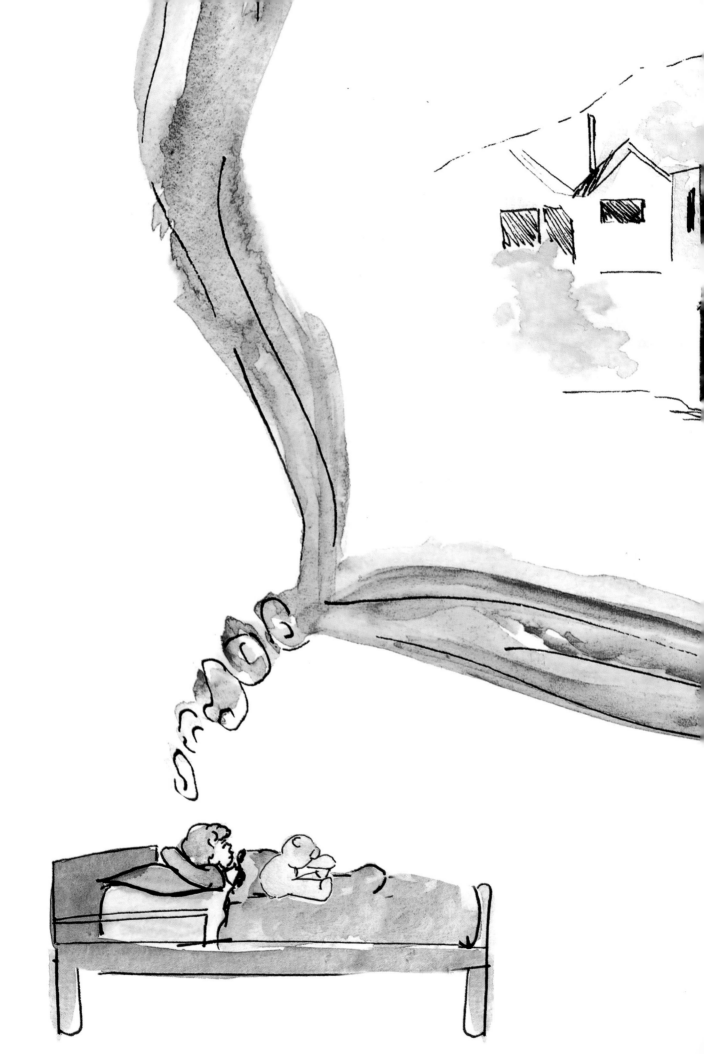

In Haiti, there are great kids
Who speak the language of fun
When your friend Pierre plays tag
You both know how to run

Although China may seem so far
Our trip would be filled with joy
Li Na would teach you yo-yo tricks
Because it's her favorite toy

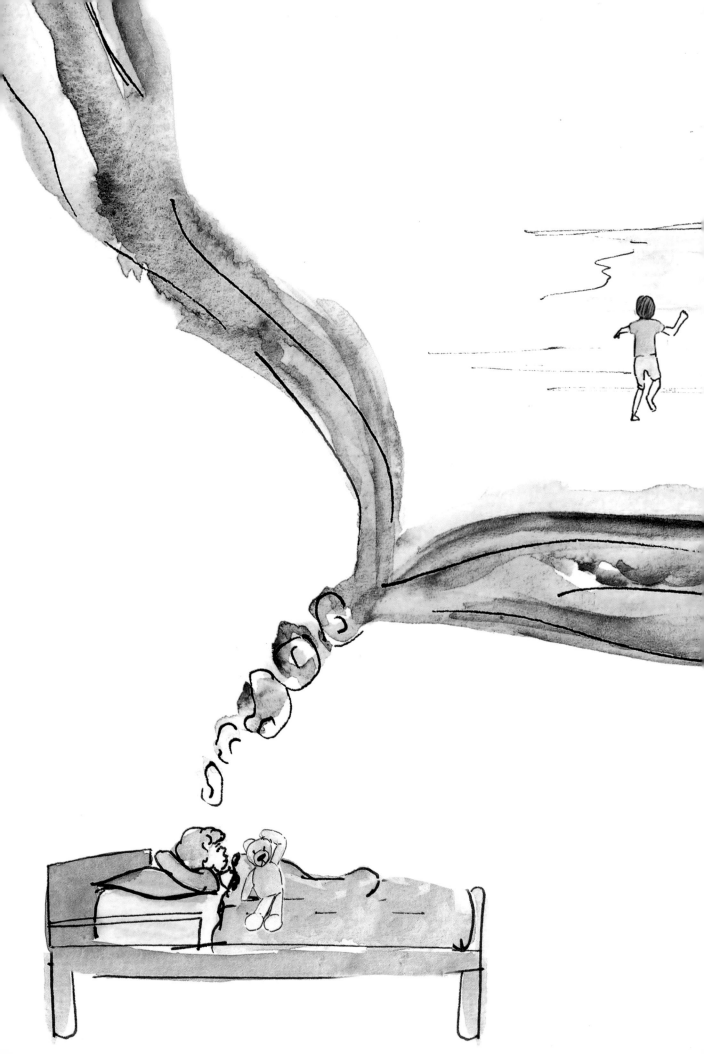

All these places have water
Whether rivers, lakes or sea
In Greece, Niko would jump with you
Over waves so wild and free."

The boy asked, "So they're just like me?
No matter where we'd go?
I thought we were so different
Are they like every kid I know?"

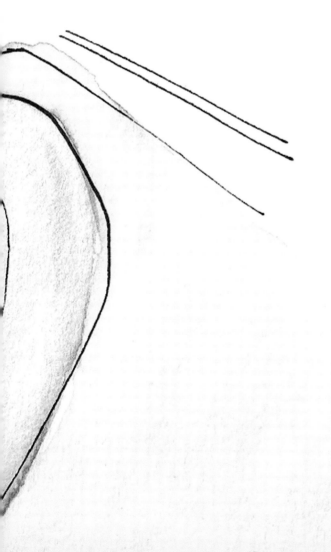

His mom said, "Kids are so alike
Each has a face and a name
Sure, they're from different places
But they're special just the same

It's easy to think of others
As just *them* from faraway
But you'd find out they're much like you
If you got the chance to play

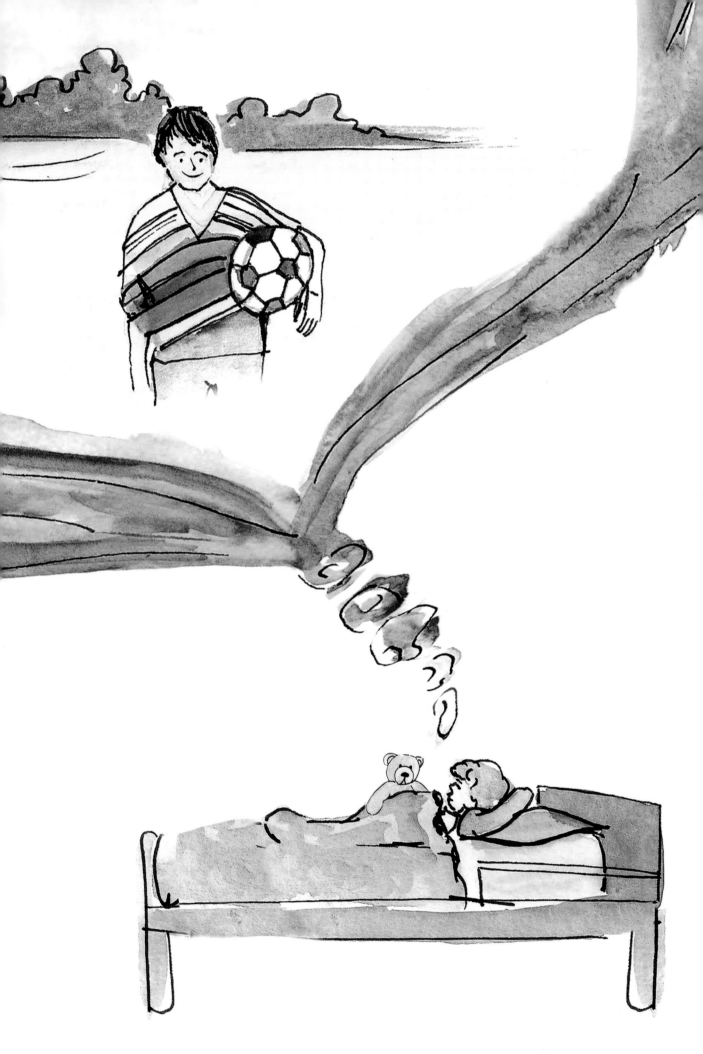

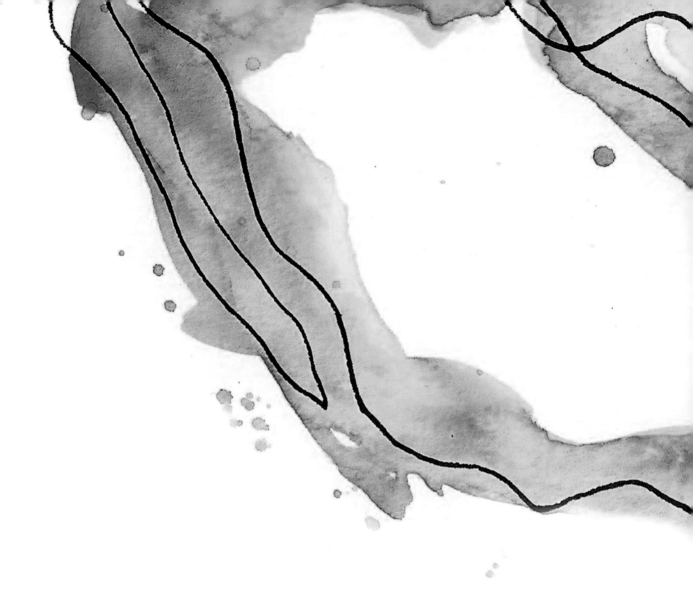

When you talk of Mexico
Picture a friend named José
He's not a *them*, he's an *us*
What would you want to say?

And although Kenya seems so far
To our hearts Zuri is near
She's not a *them*, she's an *us*
Whether or not she lives here

India has lots of kids
But picture Raj as just one
He's not a *them*, he's an *us*
He's a friend and someone's son

If Iraq goes through hard times
Let's do what we can do
'Cause Noor is not *them*, she's *us*
Maybe one day she'll help us, too

From the small island of Haiti
To China, so big in size
They're not a *them*, they're an *us*
And each kid is a prize

While we may never visit Greece
And Niko we may never see
He's not a *them*, he's an *us*
Just the same as you and me

Son, it's time for sleep now
To dream of all these places
And rather than thinking of *them*
Let's imagine real kids' faces,"

The boy thought of all these kids
As he rolled over in bed
He wished he could hug them all
So he hugged his bear instead

Then he gently closed his eyes
And pictured kids everywhere
The boy gave one more hug
As he whispered to his bear

"All kids are made special
No matter who they are
They're not a *them*, they're an *us*
Every kid, near and far."

Erin Burchik is a wife and mom who is passionate about her family, many nations, foster care and adoption. Erin works at the Grace Family of Churches in the metro Atlanta area leading international and local outreach. Erin earned her Master's Degree in Social Work specializing in Marriage and Family Therapy from the University of Georgia.

Aimee is first and foremost a lover of all things beautiful. Passiona about the role of arts in the formation of culture, she seeks to learn more about how art and beauty can both intersect and how it can impact those of all ages. A graduate of Savannah College of Art an Design, you will mostly find her sketching or lettering, painting w watercolors, or styling vintage goods.

You can see more of Aimee's work at aimeestrickland.com